CW00862947

Hands Up! at Jug

Ben didn't mean to
rector's garden. Bu
owner of the ball, C
about it, and nor can the other Handies &
Spouts. After all, they promise to go and get it
back for him straight after school.

When they can't find the ball anywhere in the
rector's garden, Hands (as they're known for
short) get him a replacement. However, Charlie
is distraught – he must have the original ball
back. So Hands are in trouble, unless they can
solve the case of the vanishing football. Ludo,
Ben and Tim suspect that the rector's son
Howard knows something about it, but Mini
won't hear a word against him. This is the third
exciting story about Hands and their adventures
at Jug Valley Juniors.

Anne Digby was born in Kingston upon Thames,
Surrey, but has lived in the West Country for
many years. As well as the *Jug Valley* books, she
is the author of the popular *Trebizon* and *Me,
Jill Robinson* stories.

Hands Up!
at Jug Valley Juniors

Anne Digby
Story devised with **Alan Davidson**

Illustrated by
Piers Sanford

PUFFIN BOOKS

PUFFIN BOOKS

Published by the Penguin Group
Penguin Books Ltd, 27 Wrights Lane, London, W8 5TZ, England
Penguin Books USA Inc., 375 Hudson Street, New York, New York 10014, USA
Penguin Books Australia Ltd, Ringwood, Victoria, Australia
Penguin Books Canada Ltd, 10 Alcorn Avenue, Toronto, Ontario, Canada M4V 3B2
Penguin Books (NZ) Ltd, 182–190 Wairau Road, Auckland 10, New Zealand
Penguin Books Ltd, Registered Offices: Harmondsworth, Middlesex, England

First published 1992
10 9 8 7 6 5 4 3 2 1

Text copyright © Anne Digby, 1992
Illustrations copyright © Piers Sanford, 1992
All rights reserved

Filmset in Monophoto Baskerville
Made and printed in Great Britain by
Clays Ltd, St Ives plc

Contents

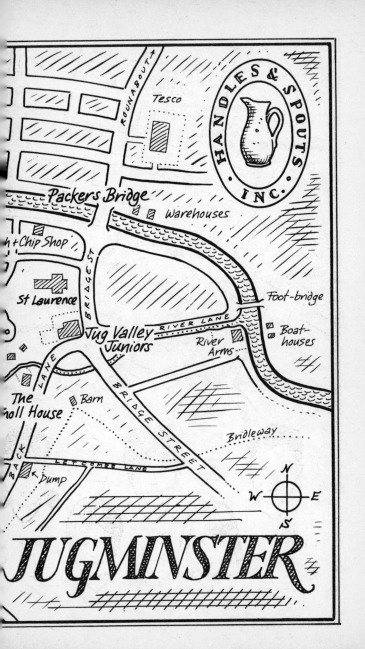

To Josh

chapter 1

Ludo Wrong

*M*ini was secretly pleased about what happened at break on the Thursday afternoon, though she wasn't going to tell the others why. It happened when Handles & Spouts were out on the school field, enjoying some sunshine after the morning's rain.

Ben kicked someone's football over into the rector's garden.

Ben wasn't pleased. It was an accident, of course.

'Now look what I've gone and done,' he groaned. 'Sorry, Charlie.'

Charlie Smith, the bottom junior concerned, was even *less* pleased. He was frantic.

'My ball!' he wailed. 'I need it! I need it! Let's run and get it back!'

But the bell had just gone.

'Don't worry!' Mini exclaimed. 'We'll go and get it back later. Promise.'

'Now!' insisted the boy, ashen-faced.

'Cool it, Charlie,' said Ben crossly. 'It's not the end of the world! Didn't you hear the bell? We'll get it back for you at home-time.'

Charlie Smith gazed at them despairingly.

Handles & Spouts wondered what the fuss was about. It was a battered old relic of a football, the worst they'd ever seen. Besides, as Mini and Ben said, they'd make sure he got it back. The five friends were in the top class at Jug Valley Juniors and four years older than Charlie. Did he think they couldn't be relied on?

Handles & Spouts Incorporated, Hands for short, was the name of their super-efficient secret club. As well as Ben Brown and Mary Minter (Mini), it comprised the twins Tim and Amy Dalladay and Ludovic (Ludo) Johnson. All five of them lived in the country town of Jugminster, close to the school, and close to each other. They held club meetings in the old yellow caravan in the Dalladays' orchard.

Retrieving a football and restoring it to its owner hardly presented a difficult challenge. It was trivial.

Of course, it mattered to Charlie Smith. The bottom junior boys were in the grips of a craze. Daily they brought their smart white footballs to school and pounded them against the rector's garden wall at playtime. The rectory wall bounded one side of the school field. Today Charlie had brought a ball, too, the best he could come up with.

The other boys had been jeering at Charlie's football. It was a very old-fashioned brown lace-up one, squashed and muddy. It was an antique. It didn't even kick properly.

'Give us a pass then, Charlie!' Ben had yelled.

As Ben's towering figure had descended amongst them, Charlie's tormentors had scattered. With a delighted grin, Charlie had tapped the ball across.

But with one hefty kick from Ben the sagging leather ball had stoved in, twisting crazily in mid-air like an old boot before shooting over the wall into the rector's garden. Ben heard it connect with something on the other side. Thud.

And then the bell had gone for lessons.

'We'll fetch it after school, Charlie,' Tim repeated as they trailed back across the

muddy field towards the class-rooms.
'Then you can take it home with you.'

'How can I?' His lower lip was
trembling a bit. 'I've got to get the bus!'

Ben and Amy exchanged rueful glances.
Of course! Was this another reason for
Charlie's agitation? Not everyone at Jug
Valley Juniors lived in Jugminster itself.
Some of them were bussed in each day,
from the outlying villages. Including
Charlie Smith, it seemed. And the school
buses that lined up at the gates, with
engines running, didn't hang around for
people who'd lost their footballs.

'Well, so what,' said Ludo, getting impatient with all this. 'You won't need it tonight! We've already said we'll get it for you. It's not going to disappear.'

'You'll have it back in the morning, first thing!' said Amy encouragingly, humouring him. 'The minute you get to school!'

'Cross our hearts and swear to die!' added Mini, looking quite gleeful.

With that Charlie Smith had to be satisfied.

'See you in the morning then, Charlie,' promised Ben, giving him a push. 'And you know the ball's bust, don't you? Well, I might try and fix it for you.'

'Thanks, Ben,' he replied grudgingly, staring at the ground and still looking worried. 'Thanks.'

He trudged off to his class-room.

'Honestly!' snorted Tim, scraping the mud off his shoes before entering the building. 'What a lot of fuss about nothing! Call that a football!'

'Grotty,' agreed Ludo.

'Never mind,' shrugged Ben. 'Guess it's the only one he's got.'

'Are you sure you don't mind, Mini?' asked Ben, pleasantly surprised.

It was home-time. Handles & Spouts were outside the main gates of JVJ, in Bridge Street. They'd just watched Charlie's bus draw away, countrywards, his face pressed palely against the window. Amy had given him a reassuring wave.

And now Mini was volunteering to be the one to go to the rectory. With Amy. It was along Bridge Street, no distance; just this side of the church.

'Of course we don't mind,' said Mini. 'Do we, Amy? If Howard's home I expect he'll help us look for it.'

Howard Kipps was the rector's son.

'Know him then?' asked Ludo in surprise.

The Rev. Kipps' son was older than them. He was golden-haired and artistic-looking and went to a private school in the town.

'Only slightly,' said Mini hastily. Amy smiled to herself.

'Well . . . great!' said Ben. It wasn't so long since he'd hit a tennis ball into the very same garden. The rector would be getting sick of the sight of him. 'Then we'll see if we can mend it or something.'

'Let's have a meeting!' Tim rapped out. He was equally pleased with Mini's

14

suggestion. He wanted to get back home and watch something on TV. 'Let's meet at HQ after tea. Spouts can collect the ball and Handles can do it up.'

'I'll bring a pump. And my puncture kit. I think they've got rubber bladders inside them, those old balls. We'll get it out and see if it's got a puncture,' said Ben.

'I'll bring some leather dubbin to clean up the case,' offered Ludo.

They agreed to meet at six o'clock. The boys turned right, towards Back Lane. The girls turned left, towards the rectory.

'What makes you think Howard's at home?' asked Amy.

'He's off school! I saw him go by after lunch, when the sun came out. He was walking the dog. He's got a sore throat.' Mini brushed her blonde fringe out of her eyes; it was getting rather long. 'He didn't come to orchestra last night.'

She was in the town's Junior Orchestra; one of the second flutes. Howard Kipps played first flute and was brilliant, according to Mini, apart from being so nice. Amy knew him only by sight so was quite curious to meet him.

'Looks as though it's going to rain

again,' she said, glancing up at the threatening sky.

They scuttled up the front path of St Laurence's rectory. It was a double-fronted Edwardian house, covered in Virginia creeper, with a big bay window each side of the front door. The front door had stained-glass panels in it and was very pretty. The panels were patterned with blue and red diamonds. Mini banged the brass knocker.

Sure enough, Howard Kipps answered the door to them. He was warmly wrapped up.

'Hello, Titch,' smiled the boy. He didn't actually know Mini's name. Yes, thought Amy, he had a very sweet face. 'Anything wrong?'

Mini was suddenly struck dumb. It was embarrassing. Amy had to do the talking.

'There's an old football in your back garden,' she said. 'One of our friends kicked it over. Can we look for it?'

Howard looked surprised. ''Course you can,' he said.

He came over the threshold and looked up at the sky. He put his hand out and made a face. 'It's nasty again, isn't it. I'd come and help you look but I'd better not.' He was apologetic. 'I'm supposed to keep warm.'

Amy was impressed by this. The boys at JVJ could take a few lessons, she thought. His hair was lovely, too, sort of gold-coloured and slightly long, curling on his neck.

'Oh, we can easily find it!' said Mini shyly, finding her voice. 'We know where it went in.'

Howard stepped back into the house.

'Dad's out but he'll be back in a minute,' he said. 'If you have any problems, I'm sure he'll help you look.' He started to close the door. 'See you, then.'

'Yes.' Mini blushed slightly. 'See you!'

The two girls hurried round the house, into a large back garden.

'Well, this should be easy,' said Amy. 'Isn't it tidy?'

The lawns were immaculate. They'd obviously been mown in the last couple of days. The high privet hedge along two sides of the garden was freshly clipped, too. Trim and neat. Although there was no sign of any clippings. The flower-beds were weeded. There were no bushes or overgrown patches that could make the search difficult.

What a contrast, thought Amy, to their wild garden at home! The garden, like the Knoll House itself, always needed things doing to it.

'What d'you think?' sighed Mini.

'He seems very nice,' agreed Amy.

'I knew he'd want to help us look for it!' said Mini triumphantly. 'Not many boys would. It's not his fault he's got a sore throat!'

'Hey! Here comes the rain now!' exclaimed Amy, glancing up. She'd just felt some drops on her hand. 'We'd better get a move on.'

They ran along below the wall, where the ball had come in. Backwards and forwards, searching anxiously. It should have been lying there on the short grass but it wasn't.

It was baffling.

And now the raindrops were getting more frequent. At the front of the house, they heard a car door slam. It seemed the rector was back.

By the time he appeared in the garden, a tall, kindly man, they'd searched everywhere.

'Not found it?' he asked.

'It's vanished, sir,' said Mini.

'Surely not,' smiled Mr Kipps. 'It's got to be here somewhere! But it's not worth getting soaked through – ' He gazed up at the black clouds. 'Look, none of us wants to get pneumonia. Run along now, before there's a downpour.'

'But – '

'Don't worry about the ball. We can have a good hunt tomorrow. Call round at the same time, yes? Now – shoo! Home! If you run all the way, you should dodge it.'

So the girls ran. And it was lucky they did. As they reached their front gates in Back Lane, the heavens opened.

'See you at six o'clock, Min!' shouted Amy through the torrential rain. She put her head down and made a dash for the Knoll House. 'Talk about it then!'

'Bye!' yelled Mini, already fumbling with her front door key at number 27 across the road. 'Bet the boys won't believe us!'

'They're going to have to! It's true!'

The Spouts were quite convinced.

Ludo had told Charlie Smith that his ball wasn't going to disappear.

Well, Ludo was wrong because it just had.

chapter 2
A Productive Meeting

'**D**on't be silly,' said Ben patiently. 'It can't have done. Not disappeared.'

'It has,' stated Mini.

'You couldn't have looked for it properly, Mini,' scoffed Tim.

'Don't start that again, Tim,' said Amy. Her brother had been getting at her all through tea. It was really annoying. 'We *did* look for it properly and it's *not there*.'

They'd all converged on HQ at six o'clock. The rain had stopped but they'd had to put on wellington boots to get there. The long grass around the caravan in the orchard was soaking wet.

Ben had brought his puncture kit and a pump. Ludo had found a tin of leather dubbin, as promised. The boys were ready to get to work on the old football. Only there was no football to get to work on. They sat around in their wet wellies, looking glum.

'Let's put our badges on,' said Mini, handing them out. 'So we can think!'

Everybody grinned.

'And I'll make some mugs of tea,' Ben suggested.

In the stillness as they waited for the kettle to boil, Tim could hear the stream rushing and gurgling outside. There were plopping sounds on the caravan's roof as water dripped off the trees. What a downpour it had been! The windows of the caravan were all steamed up.

'The rector says we can come back same time tomorrow,' Amy sighed. 'But it's useless. The ball's not there.'

Ben was beginning to look uneasy.

'Charlie's going to have a fit,' he said.

'There's got to be some logical explanation,' frowned Ludo. He was doodling in the club notebook, drawing footballs and putting faces on them. 'Let's try and think what could have happened.'

'Well, first,' said Tim, 'what could have happened is that the girls . . . ouch!'

Amy had kicked him in the shin.

'Wait!' said Ben. 'I'm just thinking.' He handed round the mugs of tea, frowning.

'What?' asked Amy eagerly.

'When I walk past with Jax sometimes, there's a dog that yaps.' Ben began to look excited. 'Hey, do they have a dog? Maybe it sank its teeth into the ball and carried it off and buried it.'

'Help!' exclaimed Ludo. 'If that's what happened, the ball's finished. I mean, really finished. That'd be the only thing to do. Give it a decent burial!'

They all laughed, even worried Ben. But Mini said, 'I've just remembered. It's a miniature poodle. It couldn't lift it.'

They sipped their tea. It was nice and hot and it warmed them up.

Ludo carried on doodling, looking bored.

'I've thought of something else,' said Ben. He frowned again. 'I'd swear the ball hit something. I heard a sort of thud. Suppose it hit a tree – ?' He brightened up. 'Suppose it got stuck in the branches of a tree and that's why the girls couldn't find it . . .'

His voice trailed off. Amy was shaking her head.

'There aren't any trees, Ben. Nothing. Just lawns and neat little flower borders.'

'The thud you heard must've been the ball hitting the ground,' Mini pointed out.

'Where is it then?' asked Ludo.

Silence.

'It's got to be somewhere,' said Tim stubbornly. He looked resigned. 'If the rector's promised to help us look tomorrow afternoon, we'll just have to go along when we get back from the class trip.'

Class 6A was going on a history trip to Jugmouth Heritage Centre.

'You lot can. I'm not too keen,' said Amy. 'It's just embarrassing.'

'And what do we say to Charlie in the mean time?' asked Ben, who wasn't too keen either.

'Oh, can't we just find him another ball?' exclaimed Mini impatiently. 'A decent one?'

The three boys looked at her.

They rose to their feet, all with exactly the same thought.

'Genius!' said Ludo. 'Yes! Why didn't we think of it? Why've we been wasting our time?'

'Dave Marshall?' said Ben. 'Dave Marshall's birthday!'

Hastily the boys unpinned their badges and flung them on the table.

'Excuse us, won't you?' laughed Tim excitedly. 'We won't be long!'

They raced out of the caravan, crossed the stream and plunged through Ludo's back garden. David Marshall lived on the same housing estate as Ben and Ludo. It was his birthday today and he'd brought a brand-new football to school. He was having a party on Saturday.

His old football was worn and battered but still much better than Charlie Smith's. He didn't need it any more. They'd offer him some cash for it!

They returned to HQ fifteen minutes later, triumphant, holding the ball.

'He let us have it for three pounds!' crowed Tim.

'It was all the money we had between us,' smiled Ludo. 'Not bad, is it?'

The girls were pleased to see Ben looking happy again. A weight had been lifted off his shoulders.

'It's good,' said Mini. Hands crowded round the ball. 'It's loads better than the one we lost.'

'What a nice surprise for Charlie!' said Amy. She hesitated. 'Shall Mini and I put in some cash?'

Mini nodded.

But the boys wouldn't let them.

'You've done enough,' said Ben. 'Going and hunting for that grotty old ball and nearly getting drenched!'

'Even though you didn't find it,' added Tim kindly. 'Spouts have spouted but Handles have handled it! We've handled the whole thing.'

'It was Mini's idea!' protested Amy, slightly nettled to see Tim so full of himself.

'Of course it was,' said Ben quickly. He

bounced the football lightly on the floor of the caravan, testing it. 'Great idea, Mini. A decent football for Charlie. This one won't get laughed at!'

'And you won't have to stick up for him any more, will you, Ben?' smiled Amy. 'You'll never have to kick his football into the middle of nowhere again!'

They all laughed.

Mini collected up the club badges and put them away in the drawer. 'See, they did help us think!' she said.

'Problem solved!' announced Ludo with satisfaction.

It had been a productive meeting, or so they thought.

chapter 3

Much Too Important

By Friday, however, they discovered
that Ben's troubles were far from over.

After the meeting on Thursday evening
Amy took the new ball indoors, to clean it
up. It wasn't leather like the old one but
vinyl. Warm soapy water was all it
needed.

'Go on, let me, Ben,' she said. 'I'll give
it you back in the morning.'

She and Mini felt the boys had been
very generous, refusing any money from
them. Of course, it was Ben who'd kicked
the old ball over the wall in the first place.
But ever since their incorporation and in
spite of their periodic arguments, Handles
& Spouts liked to stick together. Especially

when one of them was in trouble.

Harry insisted on helping her.

Harry was the twins' baby brother. He was two years old, with brown curly hair just like theirs. When he saw that Amy had a sink full of soap bubbles in the kitchen and was floating a football on it, he was thrilled. He dragged a chair across to the sink and clambered up.

'Bootfall!' he cried. He patted the ball with podgy hands, sploshing muddy soapy water everywhere.

The dirt all came off easily; most of it on to Harry.

'Right, Harry. Now see if you can find a carrier bag.'

They dried the ball and polished it with an old rag, then squeezed it into a Tesco bag. 'All clean!' said Harry.

'All ready for Charlie,' nodded Amy. 'And now it's your turn to have a bath, Harry. Come on! Before Mum sees you.'

When Ben and Ludo came to call for Tim the next morning, they gloated over the ball and its being such a bargain. Lucky old Charlie, they said.

They were late this morning. So they rushed ahead with it, along the lane. Amy and Mini met up as usual and followed along behind.

Charlie Smith was waiting at the school's
Back Lane gates. He was jumping up and
down on the spot, feeling agitated. The
school bus had dropped him at JVJ some
minutes ago. He'd raced all round the
playground, looking for Ben Brown. He
kept peering along the lane but there was
no sign of him and now the first bell had
gone.

Suddenly relief flooded through him.

He could see Ben and his friends striding
this way. Ben was swinging a carrier bag
at his side. It was bulging and football-
shaped. Hurray! They'd got it then! Now
he was safe!

'Got my ball?' he called eagerly, rushing
to meet them.

'Surprise, Charlie!' grinned Ben. He
hurled the carrier bag lightly into the air.
'Catch!'

The bottom junior boy caught the bag
cleanly. He could feel the ball plumped
up inside. He laughed with pleasure.

'You've fixed it for me?'

'Have a look in the bag!' shouted Mini,
coming up with Amy.

They all swept through the gates and
towards the school building, with Charlie

in their midst. The second bell was ringing now! Charlie scrabbled at the bag as they ran, pulling out the ball. Then he stopped dead.

Handles & Spouts stopped with him, waiting for the cry of joy.

It didn't come.

'It's different. It's not the same one,' he frowned.

'It's a present, Charlie,' Ben explained. 'It's yours. It's good. A really good kicker! We got it off Marshall for you.'

David Marshall was in the school team, and its star. He'd scored the winning goal against Jugmouth Bs, last week.

Charlie cradled the ball to his chest, fingering it. For the moment he was awestruck. He gulped. 'It's really for me? You paid for it?'

'We did.' Ben laughed. He pulled Charlie's ear. 'It's yours, OK? See you, then!'

Handles & Spouts raced forward, surging over the school threshold. They were nearly last in! Then Ben heard the strangled little cry behind him.

'Ben!'

'What's the matter now?'

Ben retraced his steps. Charlie was still

standing there in the playground, like a
statue. His face had a sort of grey tinge.

'The other ball?' he begged, tugging
Ben's sleeve. 'Where is it? I need it!'

'What for? It's lost,' confessed Ben. 'We
couldn't find it! Anyway it was bust,
Charlie!'

At that moment Mrs Edwards, who was
on playground duty, came round the corner.

'Charlie Smith! Didn't you hear the
bell? Go and put that football away and
get to assembly. You too, Ben.'

Ben caught up with the others, in the
cloakrooms.

'Everything OK?' asked Amy anxiously.

Ben shrugged. He looked uncomfortable. 'He still wants his old ball back!'

'Cheek!' glowered Tim. 'After us spending all our money!'

'Modern youth is never satisfied!' joked Ludo. But Ben just bit his lip.

'Cheer up, Ben,' said Mini. 'You've done your best. We all have. Charlie can't really want that old relic back. He'll soon forget about it.'

'And if he doesn't, too bad,' added Tim crossly.

Charlie didn't forget about the old football. He couldn't. It was much too important for that.

He was desperate to find it. At morning break he tried to sneak along to the rectory. But he was caught by Mr Gage and got a tremendous telling off. Bottom juniors were strictly forbidden to leave school premises.

Handles & Spouts were waiting for the coach to take them to Jugmouth at the time. They were hanging round the main gates, with the rest of 6A. Everyone was clutching a packed lunch and looking forward to the class trip to the Heritage Centre. 6B went last week.

Mr Gage, who was 6A's class teacher, had nipped along Bridge Street to look for the coach. Hands were startled when he reappeared with Charlie Smith.

He was marching him back to school and looking angry.

Charlie himself was fighting back tears of frustration.

'Twins. Take Charlie back to his class-room, will you. He's to stay in for the rest of playtime.' He wagged a stern finger at the boy. 'And if I ever catch you out in Bridge Street again, you'll be reported to Mr Morton.'

Once back in the empty class-room, Charlie slumped down at his desk and burst into wracking sobs.

'What's the matter, Charlie?' asked the twins, both at once, in great alarm.

'Can't we guess?' That was Ben's voice. He advanced into class 3B, Ludo and Mini just behind him. 'Oh heck.'

'Here, borrow my hanky, Charlie,' said Mini worriedly.

'I've gotta get the ball back,' sniffled the boy into Mini's pink flowered handkerchief. They all gathered round him helplessly. He raised a tear-stained face. 'It's not mine. I've gotta put it back where it came from. Before someone finds out I borrered it.'

'Oh,' said Ben glumly.

'Who did you borrow it from?' coaxed Amy. 'Can't you explain to them?'

Charlie shook his head stubbornly.

'I've gotta put it back,' he repeated. He looked scared.

'OK,' said Tim, with furrowed brow. 'We'll go back there. We'll have a *proper* look for it.'

Mini and Amy bridled at that. But hope was dawning on Charlie's face.

'Will you? Honest?'

''Course,' said Ludo.

'So you mustn't be a cry-baby,' said Ben. 'We'll find it somehow. Not right now because of getting the coach. But when we get back. At home-time. We'll go round and see the rector. It *must* be there somewhere.'

'Home-time?' gulped Charlie. He looked scared again. 'But I'll be gone by then. And –' He went even paler as he realized. 'Oh *no*! It's the weekend.'

The five friends looked at each other in despair. The coach would be arriving at any moment.

Amy knelt beside Charlie, put an arm

round his shoulders and dried his cheeks with Mini's handkerchief.

'Now, try and be brave, Charlie. Try and think sensibly. Does the person it belongs to . . . I mean it's such an old thing. Will they be needing it this weekend?'

Charlie shook his head. He'd stopped crying. He rested his elbows on the desk and dug his knuckles into his cheeks.

'Will they know it's gone?'

'They might see the bag's empty,' he muttered.

'It's kept in a bag, is it?' asked Tim eagerly. 'Well, that's easy then. How often do they get it out?'

'Not often,' said Charlie cautiously.

'Right then!' Ben slapped him on the back. 'Don't you see? What Tim means is you can put your new ball in the bag. Just for the weekend. We'll give you the old one back on Monday. OK? With luck the person won't ever know you took it!'

Relief shone on Charlie's face. Whoever this person was, he seemed pretty scared of him.

'I never thought of that!'

It was then that the coach driver sounded the horn, outside.

'They're waiting for us!' exclaimed Ludo. 'We'd better run.'

'OK then, Charlie? See you Monday!' whooped Tim.

'Think you'll find it?' asked Charlie eagerly.

'Surely!' replied Tim, over his shoulder. 'Got the whole weekend, haven't we?'

'Bye, Charlie,' Amy called. 'Got to dash!' She handed Mini her handkerchief back. It was very damp.

They left Charlie Smith sitting there in the empty class-room, depending on them, looking hopeful. To the girls it was a tragic sight.

They only wished they could share Tim's optimism.

'Well, I know one thing,' said Mini stoutly, as they scrambled on to the coach. 'It'll be nice to see Howard again. Maybe he'll have a brainwave. Maybe he'll come up with the answer to the mystery!'

chapter 4

At Last, a Clue

'**I**t's not here,' said Tim wearily. They'd been searching for the ball for half an hour. He turned to the girls. 'You were right all along,' he admitted.

They were back from Jugmouth. As well as visiting the Heritage Centre they'd walked along the windy sea front. The sea had been in wild dancing mood, grey-topped waves breaking on a sandy shore. The rain had held off all day but the wind had tangled and matted their hair.

They'd come straight to the rectory, looking dishevelled and travel-stained, especially the boys. And they were all longing for their tea! But Charlie was on their conscience.

They'd searched everywhere. The rector had tried to be helpful. There was really nowhere the ball could have gone he said but he suggested they check the hedge.

The dense, close-cropped privet was as solid as a wall. If the ball had hit it, it would more likely have bounced off, they thought. But they'd checked all along its length, poking it with sticks. The hedge ran the whole way down the garden, opposite the wall that bounded the school field, then turned and ran along the bottom of the garden.

They poked away, trying to find a hole or gap where a ball could have found entry. But it was solid. Then the boys ran along on all fours, getting muddy in the process, scanning the foot of the hedge, all the way round. Backwards and forwards they went.

Nothing.

The Rev. Kipps had long since disappeared, apologetically saying something about his car.

Howard wasn't around to have a brainwave, after all. He was better today, it seemed, and had gone to school.

'Well, I'm stumped,' said Ben. He looked glum. They all did, including the girls. They didn't even feel like crowing or saying 'we told you so'.

'A ball can't just disappear off the face

of the earth,' frowned Ludo. 'It's just not possible.'

'Looks like a case for Hands,' said Tim darkly.

'Look!' said Mini suddenly, instantly cheering up. A figure was emerging through the elegant French windows that led on to the terrace at the back of the rectory. 'Howard's back!'

'Oh?' said Ludo. 'What can he do about it?'

'Big deal!' muttered Tim.

The boy came down the terrace steps and hurried across the lawn to meet them. He was just back from school. He was wearing the Abbey School uniform, grey trousers and dark green roll-neck sweater. His golden hair framed his face. His mother's tiny poodle was under his arm. Yo-Yo always liked attention.

'No luck?' he asked.

Amy suddenly thought how messy the Handles looked, beside Howard. She felt slightly ashamed of them, with their muddy shoes and matted hair and sweaty faces. But she dismissed the thought quickly. She felt she'd been disloyal.

'Hello, Howard,' Mini said shyly. 'We *still* can't find it!'

'How odd,' he said.

The boys just stood around in silence.

'I'll have a hunt in the hedge,' said Howard helpfully.

As he took a few steps, the poodle under his arm, Tim called out, 'We've already looked.'

'Just about everywhere,' grunted Ben.

Howard rejoined them. He set the miniature dog down on the ground. 'Perhaps Yo-Yo can help find it!' he laughed.

He clapped his hands. 'Search!' he said.

The little creature just stood there, shivering.

Ben stared at the animal, thoughtfully. Was it possible? Would a dog like this have the stamina to drag the ball off somewhere? He decided to put it to the test by throwing a stick.

'Fetch, Yo-Yo!' he said.

The dog didn't show the slightest interest. It remained glued to the spot, still shivering.

'I'm afraid Yo-Yo's not the outdoor type,' said Howard, laughing even more. He scooped him up in his arms. 'He's cold. I'd better take him indoors. Then I'll come back and help you look.'

'No need, thanks,' said Ben crisply, to Mini's disappointment. 'The ball's not here. It's vanished, worse luck.'

'Let's go home,' said Tim, feeling cross.

'Just an old one, wasn't it?' asked Howard sympathetically.

His mother suddenly appeared at the French windows.

'Howard! John's on the phone. He wants to know if you're going to choir practice tonight.'

Howard, who was in the church choir, turned to Mini and gave her a really friendly smile.

'Better go. Cheer up, Titch. If it turns up, I'll let you know. Promise.'

He dashed up to the terrace and then disappeared indoors, with Yo-Yo.

Handles & Spouts left the garden via the back drive and made their way round the side of the house.

'I think Howard'll carry on trying to find it for us,' sighed Mini, 'anyway.'

'Don't be daft,' replied Tim. 'That was just smarm.'

Mini sniffed and tossed her head.

Ludo kicked the gravel on the drive. There was a gleam in his eye.

'Didn't you lot notice anything funny?'

'What?' asked Amy.

'How did he know it was an *old* ball?'

The other two boys stared at Ludo with interest, but Mini was furious.

'Because Amy told him it was, of course!' she retorted. 'Didn't you, Amy?'

'I certainly did,' replied Amy loyally.

'Lu was only asking,' rapped out Tim. '*Somebody* must have done *something* with the ball. A ball can't just walk . . .'

'And you actually think – ' Mini raised her voice angrily.

'Don't shout!' overrode Ludo. 'We don't think anything! Just checking – '

'Yes you *do* think – and stop shouting yourself – '

They were dishevelled, disgruntled – and hungry. It was all getting very heated.

'Sh!' hissed Ben suddenly, as they rounded the corner of the house. 'The rector!'

The Rev. Kipps was out at the front. He was brushing out the back of his hatchback. The tail door was up. They'd have to walk straight past him.

'Hello,' said the rector.

He straightened up, dustpan and brush in hand. He'd been bending inside the

43

back of the car, sweeping into the dustpan some bits of greenery from the rear platform.

'No ball then?' he asked kindly, looking at their cross faces. 'Now isn't that strange. It couldn't have come over here after all.'

'Anyway, thanks for letting us look,' said Ben, who knew it most certainly had.

They were squeezing past the open hatchback. Inside, Ludo glimpsed some interesting things on the rear platform. Lawn shavings, bits of twig and greenery. And, neatly folded in a pile, some empty black plastic sacks.

At the same moment, Mini was staring at the bits of greenery in the dustpan.

Privet clippings.

They both stopped in their tracks.

Ludo looked at Mini and Mini looked at Ludo. Their quarrel was instantly forgotten.

At last, a clue!

'Have you been to the dump lately, Mr Kipps?' asked Mini.

'Yesterday afternoon. Why?'

'Was that where you'd been when Amy and I called round?' she gabbled eagerly.

'Had you just bagged up a lot of rubbish from the garden? To take to the dump?' asked Ludo.

The other three had come back, to see
what was going on. They quickly grasped
the deductions that Ludo and Mini were
making.

'It is important, sir!' said Ben.

The rector found himself surrounded by
five questioning faces.

'Well, yes. I always bag the garden
rubbish. I don't think bonfires are a good
thing, do you?' The rector smiled. 'It does
make a lot of work though. Filling the
sacks, putting them in the car. Tipping
them out again, the other end. Makes a
mess, too. Stuff always tends to spill in the

45

car. But,' he sermonized, 'it's all in a good cause.'

'You didn't notice our ball did you, sir?' Amy blurted out. 'A collapsed old leather one. When you tipped the bags out.'

'Afraid not.' The rector shook his head. He cast his mind back. 'Mind you, I was in a hurry. Expecting it to rain again, y'see. Just emptied the rubbish bags quickly, one after the other.' He looked thoughtful. 'Ah, I see what you're thinking.'

'It must have been there all right!' nodded Ben.

Handles & Spouts were triumphant. It was the only possible explanation!

'You must have bagged the old ball up in the garden rubbish, sir!' laughed Tim. 'Just before my sister and her friend came round to get it.'

He turned to the others.

'Let's go to the dump and search for it!'

'Let's go straight after tea!' agreed Ben. Great – some action!

Mr Kipps was suddenly looking very doubtful.

'Doesn't work, I'm afraid,' he said regretfully. 'I filled every one of those black plastic sacks myself. Most of them

46

the day before. Tedious job. And I promise you, there was no ball there. I could have missed it when I tipped them *out*. But not when I was shovelling the stuff *in*.'

The boys exchanged thoughtful glances. The girls, impatient ones.

'I think it's still worth us looking at the dump,' said Ludo tactfully.

'Yes, by all means,' agreed the rector. 'But I don't think that can be the explanation. Alas.'

They hurried off. Once safely out of earshot, on Bridge Street, Mini started to giggle.

'We'll go to the dump, then? The minute we've had our teas! Bet you the ball's there. Blind old bat!'

Ludo opened his mouth to say something, then quickly closed it again. Instead, 'Yes, I expect the ball's there,' he stated calmly. 'That's the main thing, isn't it?'

Tim and Ben knew what Ludo was thinking. But they, too, decided to leave it at that.

chapter 5
A Secret Clash

As Charlie's football was no longer at the rectory, it had to be at the dump. Simple. They were all more or less agreed on that.

How it got there, the girls felt, was equally simple. When Ben had kicked it over it must have landed in the soft rubbish heap. The Rev. Kipps had shovelled it into one of those big black plastic sacks of his. It had been buried inside the privet clippings, the lawn shavings and the other garden refuse – and he'd missed it.

Secretly, the boys thought otherwise. Ben was sure the ball hadn't made a soft landing. And they didn't think there was anything wrong with the rector's eyesight. How could you shovel a ball up without seeing it? Different when it came to tipping it *out*, of course. Especially if you were in a hurry.

Handles had their own theory as to how the ball came to be in one of the sacks.

'I suspect malice aforethought,' Ludo told Ben, upon leaving the others.

'Me too,' agreed Ben, though he wasn't the suspicious type by nature. 'The way he laughed at us. It was a dead give-away!'

But all three boys kept their thoughts to themselves. There was no point in upsetting the Spouts. It would only lead to outpourings! Let Mini and Amy keep their illusions. Their clash of view would remain secret. At least smart detective work was leading them places. As Ludo said, that was the main thing. It looked as though the end of the trail might be in sight!

As the twins burst into the kitchen of the Knoll House, the big pot simmering on the Aga smelt at its most delicious. Mrs Dalladay was good at home-made soups. Today's was cream of tomato. It was actually intended for supper.

'Can we have some now, Mum?' begged Tim. 'We're starving!'

'And we've got to go out again after tea!' added Amy.

'OK,' laughed Mrs Dalladay. 'Go and get washed and I'll put some out for you. Sea breezes made you hungry? Had a good time?'

'Great!' replied the twins, rushing off.

They washed, changed into old clothes and put their gumboots on; ready to go straight to the dump after tea. When they came back, two steaming bowls were waiting for them on the table. Harry was banging a spoon and demanding soup, too.

'You don't like tomatoes, Harry,' Amy pointed out.

'Can you look after him tomorrow afternoon, Tim?' asked Mrs Dalladay. 'Daddy and I have got to go out. It's your turn.'

''Course I can,' said Tim cheerfully. Amy and Mini had done it last time. He was sipping down the soup with delicious mouthfuls of crusty French bread. 'Mmm. This is ace, Mum.' He looked across at Harry and grinned. 'I'll take you for a walk in the push-chair, Harry. We'll go and look at the boats.'

'Boats!' shrieked Harry joyfully.

'Where will you be going, Mum?' asked Amy with interest. 'Where's Daddy now?'

Mr Dalladay's work was home-based. He was a systems designer. He usually joined them for tea.

'He's gone to see a new client,' said Mrs Dalladay happily. 'And I've had some more work in, too.' She was a commercial artist. 'So, all in all –'

'What?'

'We've decided to go to Jugmouth and choose some carpet for the stairs, now they're fixed!'

The twins received this news with interest. The stairs had been fixed for some time. It would be nice to have them carpeted, like other people's! The Knoll House was a rambling old ruin of a place. The Dalladays were doing it up bit by bit, whenever they had money to spare. It was a slow process. Things were often rather chaotic indoors. That was why Tim and Amy had been given the old caravan, conveniently out of the way.

'Good,' said Amy. Eagerly the twins discussed what colour stair-carpet they'd like. Amy wanted pink, with big flowers. Tim favoured dark brown, so as not to show the mud. He was always being asked to take his shoes off at Ludo's house.

'But you will be back by six?' Tim asked

suddenly, remembering. 'That's when Dave Marshall's party starts.'

'Long before then,' smiled Mrs Dalladay. 'We'll only be gone a couple of hours. We thought we'd go to the Warehouse.'

The Warehouse, as it was called, was a big carpet shop in Jugmouth. Jugminster, being quite a small country town, didn't have its own carpet shop any more.

'That's OK, then,' nodded Tim with relief. He glanced at his sister. 'Ready?'

'Can we get down, Mum?' asked Amy.

Mrs Dalladay laughed. They were already half-way to the back door.

She wondered what their secret club was up to this time.

It was always interesting at the dump. It was at the far end of Back Lane, on the edge of the open countryside. It wasn't a very big one. Every so often council lorries came and took everything away to a much bigger dump elsewhere. Luckily they hadn't called since yesterday afternoon.

It was hidden behind a high hedge. As the twins cycled up they could see two bikes at the gate. Ben and Mini had just arrived. Ben was trampolining on an old

bed-frame, which had a wire-mesh base above broken springs. Mini was poking through a pile of old clothes with a stick.

The twins, turning in through the entrance, waved to them.

'Look at all these old dresses, Amy!' cried Mini. 'Some of them have got sequins on! We could use them for dressing up.'

'They're disgusting, Min!'

'This bed's good, Tim,' yelled Ben. 'Trampoline!'

With a whoop Tim ran across and took a flying leap on to the worn-out bed-frame.

'Batman . . .!'

Under both boys' weight the wire mesh collapsed with a great pinging sound. They landed on their backs, amongst the broken springs, laughing.

Amy and Mini gave the boys a hand up. They weren't hurt, though Ben's gumboot had jammed in one of the bed springs. They managed to pull it free.

'Have a sit down!' giggled Amy, struggling to up-end an armchair that lay on its side. It was a horrible old thing, with soaking wet stuffing hanging out.

'No thanks!' laughed Ben.

Tim grinned. He looked around.

'Where's Ludo, Ben?'

'He'll be here in a sec. His mum said he had to make his bed.'

'Let's start looking, anyway!'

The four of them fanned out across the dump, searching for heaps of garden refuse. Ben found a pile but it wasn't the one. It was very old and rotted down. One that the council lorries had missed, by the look of it.

Then, from behind a stack of old car tyres and broken washing-machines, came a shout from Amy.

'Here! Quick! This is the one.'

Ludo had arrived. He left his bike by the gate and came running over, holding a plastic bag for the football. It was bound to be filthy!

'Come on, Lu!' shouted Ben. 'Amy thinks she's found the rector's rubbish!'

They converged on Amy.

'Look – it's fresh!' she exclaimed. 'And there's loads of privet in it. This has *got* to be it!'

She was already scrabbling through a mass of damp lawn shavings and privet trimmings. The other four pitched in, all digging with their bare hands.

'Charlie's ball's got to be here somewhere!' said Tim excitedly. They scattered the refuse from the rector's garden in all directions, zipping through it.

'Ouch!' complained Ben, over on the far side. 'This stuff pricks!'

'What stuff, Ben?' asked Amy.

'The rector's holly.'

'Where *is* the ball?' Tim was asking in annoyance. He and Ludo started kicking at the remnants with their gumboots, getting down to bare earth. 'It's not here! There's nothing here.'

'It's *got* to be here!' said Mini, joining in the kicking. The privet and grass cuttings were scattered over a wide area now.

Of an old collapsed leather football there was no sign.

Amy looked at Ben, who was standing apart from them and sucking his hand.

'The rector hasn't *got* any holly, Ben!' she exclaimed suddenly.

'Yes, he has,' said Ben stubbornly. 'Look!'

For the first time they all realized that Ben was standing up to his ankles in holly clippings. The clippings had been on the far side of the pile, covering that bit of it.

Tim and Ludo went and stood beside him. They turned over the holly clippings with the toes of their boots. There were quite a lot of them.

'Where?' asked Tim. 'Where's the rector got any holly?'

They all thought about it. They'd searched every inch of his back garden, hadn't they? There'd been no holly in the hedge; just privet, all the way along. No holly trees. Certainly no holly bushes, either. If there had been, they'd remember having searched them.

'He hasn't,' said Amy. 'Not round the back.'

'What about the front?' asked Ben.

'No.' Mini closed her eyes, picturing it. Mini had a photographic memory, which was very useful sometimes. 'There's no hedge, just those iron palings. And no holly bushes or anything. Just some creeper growing up the house.'

'So the question is . . .' began Ludo.

'Who *has* got some?' finished Amy breathlessly.

Ludo was already crouching down. Gingerly, so's not to prick himself, he collected up a number of holly leaves and put them in his plastic bag. Samples.

'The ball's gone, hasn't it?' he said. 'So who found it? The most likely person is the person who came here *after* the rector, to dump their holly cuttings. We know they came after because – look – some of the holly's *on top* of some bits of privet.' He plucked a stem of privet from beneath the holly, to prove his point.

'They couldn't have missed the football,' nodded Mini eagerly. 'It would have been staring them in the face.'

'So they thought they might as well take it home. How are we going to find out who it was?' asked Ben, looking determined.

'Detective work, of course!' said Tim, enthusiastically. He'd been bitterly disappointed to find the ball gone. But now, thank goodness, they had a clue. A really absorbing one. 'Come on. Let's go!'

The boys had their secret view about who was to blame for all this. But they put it aside. There was work to be done. It was only later, when things got rather dodgy, that it began to matter to them.

chapter 6

House to House

'**L**et's have a meeting *right now*!' said
Tim, outside the Knoll House. They'd
been wheeling their bikes. 'Let's go down
to HQ.'

'Get your magnifying glass then, Tim,'
said Ludo.

'I'll go round to the rectory,' Mini
offered. 'Better check. Better make sure.'

'Good idea,' nodded Ben. 'Any clipped
holly in the front garden and we're wasting
our time.'

'I'm sure we're not!' Mini called over
her shoulder as she pedalled off. Amy
smiled to herself. She guessed her best
friend was hoping to catch a glimpse of
Howard Kipps; hoping he'd smile from one
of the windows? Give her a friendly wave?

Tim was already racing indoors to find
his magnifying glass.

Turning into Bridge Street, Mini realized something.

Howard might be at church by now. Choir practice. Mini had a good voice herself; she was in the school choir. Lately she'd been wondering whether to join the church choir, too. No particular reason. She hadn't been able to make up her mind about it.

She dismounted. Slowly she wheeled her bike along the pavement, past the frontage of St Laurence's rectory. She checked very carefully as she went, peeping through the iron palings. No holly anywhere. Not a scrap. So her photographic memory hadn't let her down. She lingered, just for a few moments. In case. Howard might wander out and say 'hello'.

But he didn't.

'No holly at the rectory!' she told the others, when she got back to the caravan.

They nodded. There was an air of excitement. They'd spread the holly leaves out on the table. They'd been examining them through the magnifying glass.

'We're in business, Mini!' said Ludo. He handed her the magnifying glass. 'Take a look.'

There were tiny flecks of black on some of the leaves.

Also, one or two of them were badly stained. Mini, quick-witted as ever, said, 'Car exhausts! So the holly grows at the front of someone's house, not the back. Quite near the road. A front hedge?'

They all cheered her.

'Good job, isn't it?' grinned Ben. 'Gives us more chance.'

'It's not going to be easy though, is it,' frowned Mini, 'finding it?'

'A challenge,' stated Ludo. 'Find a front garden with a newly-clipped holly hedge. Or bush.' He turned over one of the leaves with his fingertip. 'At least very few people have them. And this is a weird kind of

61

holly. Look at the funny little veins.' He sighed. 'Big job, though. We're talking about a house-to-house search.'

'Well, garden to garden,' said Mini.

'Lucky we've got the whole weekend,' remarked Tim. 'That's all I can say.'

'It'll be worth it!' retorted Amy, hoping Tim wasn't losing his resolve. She was still haunted by that scared look on Charlie Smith's face. 'The person with the holly's most likely got the ball. If we find the right front hedge, we find Charlie's ball!'

'And then we'll explain, won't we?' said Mini. 'And beg 'em to give it back.'

Ben nipped home and got some of his mother's transparent freezer bags. He knew she kept them in the kitchen drawer. He came back, sorted the holly leaves into five piles then carefully sealed them in the five polythene bags. One bag each. Samples to work from. Now they could handle the leaves and look at them without getting pricked.

'That's clever, Ben,' said Amy.

In the mean time, Tim went indoors and located the Dalladays' small street map of Jugminster. His father was just back, and let him run some copies off on the photocopier.

'Good stuff!' said Ludo, when he returned. 'One each.'

'And one for HQ,' replied Tim. He stuck it up on the wall with some Blu-tack. 'Command and control centre.'

Ludo picked up the pencil. He peered at his own map through his reddish fringe.

'Now. The earliest we can start is after lunch tomorrow.' They all had clubs at JVJ on a Saturday morning. 'We'll need to take our bikes and fan out. We'd better split the town into five sections. Take one section each.'

Their street maps of Jugminster were lying in front of them. They realized it was going to be a huge task.

'Hey, you can't take your bike, Tim,' Amy reminded him. 'You'll have Harry some of the afternoon.'

'You're right,' Tim realized. He frowned at his map. 'That means I'll have to push him round in the push-chair with me.'

'Look, Tim, you take these streets here,' said Ben helpfully. 'They're easy. They're all little streets.' He was prodding Tim's map. 'Not far to walk, either.'

The network of small streets in question lay just the other side of Packers Bridge. Everyone agreed that this could be Tim's area. Then they divided up the rest of Jugminster between them and marked their maps accordingly. Ben said he'd do the most far-flung bit.

They laid their plans. They'd set off separately, after lunch the next day, each making their own way, each keeping to their own area. They'd spend two or three hours combing their section of the town, then report back to HQ.

'At four o'clock,' suggested Tim. '1600 hours. Back to HQ for a progress report. In case one of us has found it.' And in case Mum and Dad are back and I can dump Harry, he thought privately.

'Yes, we might've done it by then,' agreed Amy.

'We'll need these then,' said Ben, handing round the samples. 'It's got to be exactly the right sort of holly. It's got to match.'

They took their transparent bags, picked up their maps and then agreed that the meeting was closed. Tomorrow afternoon, the house-to-house search would begin.

It had seemed so trivial, Ben kicking the collapsed old ball over the rectory wall. Instead, it was turning into one of their most challenging cases ever.

chapter 7

Positive Sighting

'**B**oats?' asked Harry in disappointment.
'More boats?'

'Later,' said Tim. 'More boats on the
way back, Harry.'

He'd given Harry less than five minutes
on Packers Bridge. The River Jug flowed
through the centre of the town. On
Saturday it was always alive with boats,
mostly sailing vessels and cabin cruisers.
Some of them would be making their way
to the wide river estuary at Jugmouth.
Like Harry, there was nothing Tim loved
better than to stand on Packers Bridge and
watch them coming through. But today he
had work to do.

He strode over the bridge to the far side,
pushing Harry's push-chair ahead of him.
The little boy was securely strapped in.
They crossed Cheap Street at the

pedestrian crossing then plunged into the network of small streets beyond.

Tim had already kept his eyes open for holly, all the way along Bridge Street. Now, striding up Pretoria Terrace, he continued to do so. The rows of terraced houses had tiny front gardens. Very few of them had hedges at all. Harry bounced up and down happily in the speeding push-chair.

'We've got to find Charlie's football, Harry,' confided Tim. 'There's this boy, you see. We think he nicked it. We think he put it with his dad's rubbish. His idea of a joke. But now we reckon someone else has got it. We think they picked it up at the dump.'

It was very complicated.

'Bootfall,' replied Harry, only grasping the first bit.

As they turned into Westbury Street he saw some boys playing with one.

'Bootfall!' he screamed excitedly.

'No!' Tim laughed. 'We're not looking for a football.'

Harry craned his head round and gazed up at Tim, blinking and perplexed.

Tim stopped and took the polythene bag out of his pocket. He squatted beside the push-chair.

'See these leaves, Harry? They're very important. You can look after them for me. That's it.' Harry took the bag in his podgy hand and held it in his lap. 'They won't prick. Hold the bag. We mustn't lose it.'

Harry nodded. He peered down at the leaves with interest.

'OK. We've got to find some like this. Holly leaves. They'll lead us to the football. Get it?'

Harry nodded again. But he hadn't really got it. He was confused.

However, he watched with interest when

Tim borrowed the bag from him in
Windermere Place. Tim was stooping by a
green bush and comparing the leaves.

'No good,' Tim sighed. He straightened
up and handed it back to his little brother.
'Wrong sort of holly. Hasn't been clipped
anyway. Got to be clipped.'

'Tree,' said Harry.

Tim trudged on. His arms were starting
to ache from pushing.

'Getting boring, isn't it, Harry?' he said
darkly. 'Howard Kipps ought to be doing
this, not us. I'd like to zap him one!'

Another four streets to go. Green began
to blur into green. Privet, hawthorn,
privet. No holly. Tim started to think
about David Marshall's party. He was
looking forward to it.

'Tree!' said Harry, every time they
passed a hedge.

'Maybe we're wasting our time,'
muttered Tim. 'Maybe the others have
found it somewhere else. Wonder if they
have?'

They hadn't. Amy and Mini had drawn a
blank. As had Ben and Ludo.

The latter had set off early. By half-past
three, in different parts of the town, they

were utterly fed up. They'd been cycling round fruitlessly for two and a half hours.

Ben got back first. Ludo found him sitting on the steps of the caravan, staring at the swollen stream. They exchanged 'thumbs-down' signs. Ben started banging himself on the head with Tim's football, which he'd found in the orchard.

'Feeling that hopeless?' grinned Ludo.

'Just trying something,' said Ben. 'Hey, I've got an idea, Lu. Give this a punch, will you?'

He lobbed the ball up into the air. As it came down, Ludo punched it away. Thud.

'That's it!' Ben exclaimed. 'That could've been the sound I heard!'

'In the garden?' asked Ludo with interest. 'When you booted Charlie's ball over?'

'Yes. It connected with something really hard. But there wasn't anything hard for it to connect with, was there? Somebody punching it away. Or even kicking it. That's what I must have heard.'

'Howard Kipps again,' mused Ludo.

'Well, I'm sure it wasn't the rector!' said Ben.

'It might have been coming straight at

him,' continued Ludo. 'So he punched it away and then decided to get his own back! It all fits, doesn't it? It all fits with what we've decided already.'

'Yes, Lu. He put it in one of his dad's rubbish bags. Now we know for sure.'

'Well, we don't know *that* for sure,' cautioned Ludo. 'It's the obvious thing, that's all. He might possibly have done something else with it.'

'Shouldn't think so – but you know what?' said Ben. He held up his fist. He was clenching it tight. 'If nothing comes of this holly business, I wouldn't mind going round and seeing him. Give him a punch, for Charlie.'

'Sh!' warned Ludo. 'The girls!'

Amy and Mini came trudging down through the orchard. Their dejected faces told their own story.

'It's like looking for a needle in a haystack,' said Mini bitterly, as they joined the boys.

'We haven't had any luck either,' sighed Ludo.

'What were you two talking about?' asked Amy.

'Oh, nothing,' Ben muttered, not meeting her eye. He stared towards the house. 'Tim's not back, then?'

'Perhaps he's found it,' said Ludo.

'Let's hope so,' replied Ben.
'Otherwise . . .'

'Otherwise what?' asked Mini.

'We might have to think of something else,' said Ben.

Amy and Mini exchanged puzzled glances and shrugged.

But at the very last, the holly hedge turned up.

It was an amazing stroke of luck. Tim could easily have missed it.

Coming along Paice Street, not far from Packers Bridge, he suddenly halted the push-chair and put the brake on. He'd just seen the time. It was four o'clock! He was supposed to be back at HQ.

'I'm hot, Harry,' he grumbled. 'We're going to have to run like the blazes in a minute. I'll just take my sweater off.'

Harry's push-chair was parked against a low garden wall. It was in front of number 38 Paice Street. The wall had a fence above. But there was a gap between wall and fence. Harry stared through the gap. It was exactly at push-chair-person's eye-level.

As Tim struggled to pull his sweater over his head, he heard Harry say, 'Tree!'

71

'Don't be silly, Harry,' said Tim. He'd got the sweater off now. He was tying it round his waist, by the arms. 'That's not a tree. It's just an old fence. Come on, we've got to run.'

'Tree! Bootfall!' shouted Harry indignantly. He thrust his podgy hand through the gap and instantly withdrew it. 'Owwwwwh!'

He'd pricked his hand.

'Harry?'

Tim squatted down and rubbed Harry's hand, at the same time squinting through the gap in excitement.

There was a holly hedge in there, growing all along the garden frontage. It would until recently have been visible from the street . . . its lower stems burgeoning out through the gap and over the pavement, its upper ones rising above the fence. But it had all been severely cut back.

It was newly clipped.

'Give us the samples!' said Tim eagerly, snatching the bag from Harry's lap.

Quickly he compared the leaves. They were identical!

'We've found it, Harry. We've found it!'

The garden gate was open. Tim wheeled

the push-chair up to the front door and knocked loudly. His heart was thudding. Would Charlie's football be here? And if so – would they give it back?

No reply. So he knocked again.

'They're out,' said the next-door neighbour, looking over the dividing fence. She was friendly, the chatterbox type. 'They've just gone up to the school. With their little girl. Minster Juniors, that's where they've gone. They said they'd be back in half an hour.'

'Thanks!' said Tim. 'I'll come back.'

Just time to get to HQ and tell the others, he thought. Then they could all come back together. Safety in numbers. They mustn't mess this up. He couldn't wait to tell them the news. One holly hedge. Positive sighting.

'Brill, Harry! You're a brill detective!' He ruffled the curly head. His brother chuckled and banged his hands together. He could tell that Tim was extremely pleased with him.

As they raced home over Packers Bridge and along Bridge Street, the push-chair flew ahead of Tim like a winged chariot. His arms didn't ache a bit, not now. Harry squealed with pleasure. It was the best ride he'd ever had.

He even forgot about the boats.

chapter 8

A Door is Slammed

*M*elissa Pugh, aged seven, felt very proud as she left the school hall. Melissa, who lived at number 38 Paice Street, went to Minster Juniors, the town's other junior school. They played netball and football matches against JVJ and the rivalry between the two schools was often bitter.

Melissa ran back to the school gates where her parents were waiting for her. They'd parked the car in the abbey close. Mrs Pugh was pleased to see Melissa looking flushed and happy. 'Did you leave it then?' she asked.

'Yes!' Then Melissa gave her father a hug. 'Thanks, Dad. You did it up really great. Teacher was ever so pleased with

me. Some of the top juniors asked where you'd found it!'

'Let's get home then,' said Mr Pugh, a grumpy man, but devoted to his daughter. 'I'm missing my programme.'

As they drove back towards Paice Street, Melissa snuggled in the back seat of the car. After days of agony, everything had turned out all right in the end. She'd been constantly nagging Mum and Dad to give her something to take. Everyone else in the class had brought something! Then, after endless silly jokes about how they needed all their old junk because they were

sitting on it or wearing it, her parents had
finally turned up trumps.

'Nice little find, wasn't it?' grunted Mr
Pugh, as they turned into Paice Street.

Handles & Spouts cycled over Packers
Bridge in a state of high excitement.
They'd left Harry with Mr and Mrs
Dalladay, who'd just got back from
Jugmouth.

'Look at his rosy cheeks, Tim!' Mum
had exclaimed. 'Been for a lovely walk?'

'You bet, Mum!' Tim had replied,
before dashing down the garden to find
the others.

Now the five of them were making all
speed towards the house with the newly-
clipped holly hedge. Good old Tim! Good
old Harry! Had they reached the end of
the trail at last?

Were their deductions going to be
proved correct?

And if so would the person who found
the football give it back?

'That's the house – that one there,' said
Tim, pointing. Having dismounted in
Paice Street, they stood holding their bikes.
'Look, there's a car outside now. They
must be back.'

'Who's going to ask?' said Ben, licking dry lips.

'Mini's good at getting round people,' grinned Ludo.

'OK,' agreed Mini.

They parked their cycles and surged up to the front door together. They could see a TV set flickering in the lounge. The set was on loud and Mini had to bang the door-knocker hard.

'All right. All *right*. I'm coming,' shouted a grumpy voice.

The front door opened but only half-way. It wasn't very welcoming. Mr Pugh peered at them, small and unshaven. A girl with straggly hair could be glimpsed in the hall behind him.

'What?'

Mini swallowed.

'Sorry to disturb you, sir. But have you found an old football?'

'What d'you want to know that for?' he snapped.

'Because we've lost one!' said Ben firmly, refusing to be intimidated.

'It's *my* football, Dad! You gave it to me!' Melissa said in panic, grabbing her father's elbow.

'Don't worry.' He shook her off. 'Get

inside, girl. Leave this to me.'

'So you *did* find it!' exclaimed Tim excitedly.

'What if I did?' asked Mr Pugh. 'Finders keepers. Ever heard of that?'

The five friends exchanged looks that were a mixture of jubilation and alarm. Jubilation that their detective work had proved to be so brilliant. Alarm that the man had given the ball to his little girl. The situation was looking distinctly dodgy.

'It's very important we have it back!' Tim blurted out.

'*Very* important,' said Amy.

'Oh, it is, is it?' said Mr Pugh. He still hadn't opened the door fully. He looked at them suspiciously. He hadn't worked so hard on the football just to give it to these herberts! He wasn't going to see his Melissa made miserable. Who were they? 'I get it,' he laughed suddenly, in relief. 'You've just come from the school, haven't you. Just trying it on, aren't you?' He gave a menacing smile. 'Tell me a bit more about this football of yours, then. Tell me where it came from.'

'From the dump!' exclaimed Mini, angrily.

78

'Don't be cheeky. Everybody knows that by now. What I mean is, it must have a very interesting story. A football like that. You must know its whole story.'

'What story?' asked Tim. He looked perplexed. 'It's just an old football.'

'Nothing special,' added Ben. 'We just want it back, please. We –'

He got no further.

'You know even less about that football than I do! Nothing special, eh? GERONOUT-OF-IT!' shouted Mr Pugh, losing his temper. 'If you really want it, you can go along and bid for it tonight. With the rest!'

The door was slammed shut in their faces.

chapter **9**

Spouts Simmer

'**S**o we were right about everything!' said Tim, as they picked their bikes up. 'It *was* in one of the rector's rubbish bags! It *did* end up at the dump. And the person who came next with the holly cuttings, *did* find it! Only snag is, we still haven't got it back.'

'After all our hard work!' exclaimed Amy in bitter disappointment.

'We weren't quite right about *everything*, were we Ludo?' said Mini, unable to resist it. 'Like your brilliant idea that Howard could have walked off with the ball. Honestly!' Even now, it still rankled.

'I wonder what that man was on about?' muttered Ben, deciding to ignore Mini's remark. 'What's so special about Charlie's football?'

'He thought we were from Minster

Juniors, didn't he?' nodded Tim, wrinkling up his nose at the very idea. 'He thought we'd heard about the ball and were just trying to con him. He was sort of testing us . . .'

'And what was that about bidding for it tonight?' interrupted Mini. 'Bidding for it where?'

All this time, Ludo had been silent. His brow was furrowed.

'I think I can answer that one,' he said.

He recalled seeing a notice in the fish and chip shop window.

They cycled straight there; back over

Packers Bridge and round the corner on to The Waterfront. They left their bikes in a cycle rack.

'Oh no, I don't believe it!' groaned Tim, as they gathered outside the shop's plate-glass window. 'They *have*! They've put it in an auction!'

It was just a small handbill, amongst several others. But Ludo never missed much. It said:

MINSTER JUNIORS PTA
will be holding

A GRAND AUCTION

Lots of lovely junk!
SATURDAY 7 P.M. * SCHOOL HALL
[In Aid of New Games Strip]

'So her dad gave it to her to give the school!' Amy realized, in despair. 'No wonder she was so upset.'

'And no wonder he couldn't give it back to us, even if he'd believed us, which he didn't!' cursed Ben. 'Oh heck, I've had it now! And so has Charlie.'

He stood there, shoulders slumped, scowling. Tim and Ludo were already walking slowly back to the cycle rack, talking together.

'Hey!' shouted Amy, suddenly grabbing Ben's arm. 'I've got it! Why don't we go to the auction and bid for it?'

'That's right!' Mini clapped her hands in excitement. 'Why not? Let's do exactly what the man said!'

'I know you'll be at the party, Ben. But Mini and I could go!' said Amy. 'We really could, couldn't we, Min?'

'No, you couldn't!' exclaimed Ludo, rushing back. He and Tim had overheard. 'You two aren't going to the auction!' he said, before Ben could make any response.

'We wouldn't hear of it, would we, Ben?' said Tim pointedly. 'Give money to Minster Juniors? For new games strip! They're conceited enough already!'

'It'd be against our deepest principles,' said Ludo.

'I'm broke, anyway,' sighed Ben, getting a word in at last.

'We all are,' agreed Ludo. 'We couldn't be broker.'

'Besides, we've bought Charlie one football already,' said Tim indignantly. 'We're not going to buy him another.'

*

The boys rushed off after that, leaving the girls feeling very annoyed.

They had to go help Ludo choose a birthday card for Dave, they said. Urgent.

'I could buy the football!' Amy had protested to them. 'I've got some money saved up.'

'Me too,' said Mini. 'I've got some money on me right now. Anyway, it'll go cheap. It's so grotty.'

'I expect that man's done it up,' Ben pointed out, 'like we were going to.'

'Even done up, I mean!' said Mini scornfully.

'Go on, Ben, let us,' said Amy. She could see he was torn. 'We didn't put anything towards the other one. Let's take a vote on it!'

'No time!' Ludo cut in quickly. 'Anyway, I think there's more to Charlie's football than meets the eye. That's what that man was trying to tell us. It's going to be expensive!' There was a gleam in his eye.

'Bound to be!' Tim chipped in. 'And what about our principles? Come on, Ben,' he said sharply. 'We'll miss the shop.'

'Think about it, Ben!' Amy called out helplessly, as the boys cycled off, along The

Waterfront, in the direction of the card shop.

The girls wheeled their bikes homeward along Bridge Street, very disgruntled. Mrs Dalladay had invited Mini back for a meal tonight but it wasn't till six o'clock. There was no need to hurry.

'I think we should have taken a vote on it,' grumbled Amy. 'I think Ben was quite keen.'

'Now the other two will get at him,' said Mini.

She slowed to snail's pace as they passed the rectory, hoping to catch a glimpse of Howard. But there was no sign of him.

'I bet Howard wouldn't have given up so easily,' she said. 'It's *our* money, after all. We can go to the auction if we jolly well want to.'

'Tim's got to come back home before he goes to Dave's party,' Amy realized. 'He's got to get washed and changed. We'll go to work on him!'

'Stick his head under water while he's washing his face!' suggested Mini.

But they had great difficulty catching Tim at all.

He raced into the Knoll House at ten to six, straight upstairs to get washed and

85

changed and then straight out again. Amy caught him flying out of the kitchen door, all spruce and cheerful looking. She seized his arm.

'We still think we should have taken a vote on it, Tim! Ben was keen.'

'Definitely!' agreed Mini.

'Waste of time! Ben won't hear of it! Not now he's thought. Honest!'

'What are we going to do, then?' asked Amy. She knew Tim wouldn't be making it up about Ben. 'What are we going to say to Charlie, on Monday?'

'This is something for Handles to handle, Amy! Ben wants to sort things out with Charlie himself! OK?' He pulled his arm free. 'Let go of me, Amy. I'm late. Got to rush!'

He raced off down the garden, leaving two simmering Spouts behind.

Mrs Dalladay had cooked a good curry but they didn't enjoy it very much. Afterwards, they offered to wash up. Amy washed and Mini dried. Mr Dalladay stayed a while, to put things away.

With sinking heart, the girls watched the hands of the big kitchen clock creep round. It was almost seven o'clock.

'Auction'll be starting in a minute,' whispered Amy fiercely, when Dad went out. He'd gone upstairs to read Harry a story. They were alone at last. Mum was in the big sitting-room, watching TV. 'You know something, Mini? I'm surprised at Ben, I really am. I know we hate Minster Juniors, but honestly!'

'The boys are standing on their dignity!' said Mini, hanging the tea-towel in front of the Aga, to dry. 'Just because we're in a position to buy the football back and they're not! What a time to be pigheaded! How can Ben *possibly* sort things out with Charlie?'

'He can find out from Charlie who the ball really belonged to and then go and explain. That's all. That's what Tim means, I suppose,' Amy reflected. 'Oh, how embarrassing. Poor Ben.'

'That's not sorting anything out! That's not going to bring the football back, is it?' said Mini angrily. 'Poor Ben? Poor Charlie, more like it!'

Amy hardly needed reminding.

Spouts hadn't enjoyed their meal this evening because they'd felt choked, every time they thought about Charlie Smith yesterday morning. Sitting there in the class-room at JVJ, half scared, half hopeful. Thinking Handles & Spouts were going to find the lost football for him and bring it back on Monday. The wrong one sitting in the bag all weekend, Charlie no doubt scared out of his wits that the owner would find out.

'Exactly seven o'clock,' said Amy, staring at the kitchen clock. 'Auction must be starting right now.'

'And once that football goes, it's gone,' said Mini, 'for ever and ever and ever.'

The two friends stared at one another, hearts bumping. Each knew exactly what the other was thinking. They didn't really have any choice, did they? Blow the Handles!

'Come on, Mini!' said Amy urgently. 'What are we waiting for?'

chapter 10

A Frantic Bid

So while the boys fed their faces and
enjoyed the celebratory mood at David
Marshall's party, the girls sped across town
to Minster Juniors in desperate haste.
They'd told Mrs Dalladay they felt like
some fresh air. Amy had raced up to the
bedroom and grabbed her money-box.

'Surely we won't need that, Amy?' Mini
had whispered. 'I've got four pounds on
me. Come on, it's *started*!'

It was just for insurance, Amy said. Both
girls expected the ball to go cheap,
whatever Ludo said. It was grotty. He'd
just been trying to put them off! They
couldn't get over it. How pigheaded the
boys were being about the auction. Well,
they'd show them! They were furious that
they'd nearly allowed themselves to be
frightened off.

The only thing that frightened them now was the time.

It was twenty-past seven when they parked their bikes at Minster Juniors. They were gulping and gasping for breath. The school hall was packed out with people. They had to push and jostle their way in, to get a place at the back. The pound coins in Amy's money-box rattled and jangled as they went.

'We'll have to stop here!' whispered Amy. They were squashed against a pillar and couldn't get any further. Amy had a fairish view from here. Mini, being tiny, less so. Were they in time? Had the football been auctioned yet?

The auctioneer was Mr Bergman, a big genial man with a red face, in charge of sport at Minster Juniors. He was just knocking down a pair of book-ends for two pounds. He was surrounded by a heap of bric-à-brac yet to be sold: piles of books, saucepans, lampshades, broken toys, dinner plates, even an old fridge. Amy scanned the heap fearfully, looking for some sign of Charlie's ball.

'Now, what next?' said Mr Bergman, as a lady beside him took two pounds from someone and handed over the book-ends.

She was the treasurer of the PTA. 'What have we here?'

He was bending down and rooting behind the fridge. Then he straightened up, holding something high above his head, balanced on the palm of one hand.

'Now here's an interesting relic,' he boomed.

Amy nudged Mini hard. 'It's the football!' she gasped.

'Phew!' said Mini. 'We're only just in time, then. It's got to be fate!'

They were *meant* to come. They were *meant* to get it.

'A bit past its best, I grant you,' the auctioneer was saying cheerily, to laughter from the audience. 'What they call a golden oldie. Footballs used to look like this once, y'know . . .'

He twirled it on his big palm, to show it off. The girls stared at it, mesmerized. Ben was right about the man doing it up. It still sagged a bit but all the mud had been cleaned off the brown leather casing. As Mr Bergman twirled it, a long faded squiggly mark on one side of the ball came into view.

'And, as you can see, this ball's been signed. It's very faint but you can still read the name. This ball's been signed at some time or other by the great, the one and only, *Joe Jackson*.'

Amy and Mini exchanged looks of alarm. Who was Joe Jackson? Did that make Charlie's ball valuable after all?

But the audience appeared not to have heard of him, either. They stared blankly.

However, Mr Bergman knew his job, which was to try to whip up excitement about his wares in order to get the best possible price for them!

'Now, you ignorant lot. No old-timers here? Everybody knows that Joe Jackson was the best footballer ever to come out of Jugminster . . .'

'The only one!' shouted a humorist in the audience.

'. . . and he played for England not once, not twice, but three times! So what am I bid for this wonderful old football?'

'I bid fifty pence!' laughed a fat lady near the front.

All around was jollity and fun. But Amy and Mini suddenly paled as they realized the significance of this new information.

The man who'd found the ball at the dump had hinted that the ball was special. And so it was. Not to most people, maybe. But to its actual owner a ball like this could be very special indeed, priceless even. Maybe of great sentimental value.

Why else would they have kept it all these years?

But Charlie Smith had borrowed the ball from that actual owner, without permission. No wonder he was so scared!

Did he know that it was a very special ball? That it was perhaps, to someone, irreplaceable? He must do! It explained everything.

And Ben had gone and kicked the ball over the rector's garden wall! Ben had gone and lost it!

Mini was gripping Amy's arm so hard that it hurt.

'We've *got* to get it now. We've *got* to. If Handles knew this they'd *want* us to. They'd forget all about their silly principles. Quick, Amy!' she hissed. 'Quick. Bid. *Bid*. Stick your hand up! They'll see you better than me.'

'Fifty pence, I'm bid. Any advance on fifty pence?'

Tremblingly, Amy raised her hand up high above her head. She'd never bid at an auction before!

'One pound. One pound at the back there.'

The fat lady who'd shouted 'fifty pence' put her hand up.

'One pound fifty in the front here. Anybody for two pounds?'

Amy's hand went up again.

'Two pounds. Two pounds I'm bid at the back.' The auctioneer looked round the hall. The fat lady had dropped out of the bidding. 'Are we all done at two pounds then . . .?'

Mini nudged Amy in excitement and glee.

But then, suddenly, a different hand went up. Someone was standing just by the fat lady. He looked from the back like a typical football supporter – a short man wearing a flat cap and muffler, with the collar of his raincoat turned up.

'Ah,' beamed Mr Bergman. 'Two pounds fifty in the front – '

Amy's hand went up.

'Three pounds at the back. Any advance – ?'

Flat-cap stuck his hand up again.

'Three pounds fifty . . .'

'Four pounds!'

'Four pounds fifty . . .!'

'Five. That's more like it!' He beamed in Amy's direction and then in Flat-cap's.

'Are we all done at five pounds then? How about you, sir? Are you the young gentleman who telephoned me earlier? You can't give up now, sir!'

Flat-cap's hand went up again.

'Five pounds fifty,' rapped Mr Bergman in delight. There was an interested hush in the hall now. Neither Amy nor Mini even noticed. They had to get the ball – they *had* to! It would be terrible if it went to that horrid little man, that horrid, hateful little man, trying to buy *their* ball.

'Six pounds I'm bid at the back!'

'Six pounds fifty . . .'

Amy's adrenalin was flowing, she was getting carried away. It was all happening so fast. *They had to have that ball!*

'Seven pounds at the back. Any advance, sir – ? Yes. Seven pounds fifty . . .'

The price was climbing into the stratosphere.

Suddenly it had reached thirteen pounds fifty.

A horrible, trembly feeling came over Amy. She had exactly ten pounds in her money-box. With Mini's four, that made fourteen. She didn't even stop to think about what this was costing – all the money she'd saved up and four pounds of Mini's as well! Only that this was *it*, then. This would be their last frantic bid and everything depended on it.

Amy's hand went up for the very last time.

'Fourteen pounds.'

And so did Flat-cap's.

'Fourteen pounds fifty I'm bid in the front here. Any advance on fourteen-fifty? Any advance – ?'

Silence. The girls just stared miserably down at the floor, their hands hanging at their sides. They'd lost.

'Going to the gentleman in the front

then at fourteen pounds fifty. Going. Going. Gone!'

And Charlie's football was knocked down to Flat-cap, who at once raced forward to pay for it.

There was a round of applause in the hall. But Amy and Mini had already turned away and were pushing their way out at the back. One or two people patted them on the shoulder as they passed, and said, 'Oh, bad luck!' and, 'Well tried!' They could see how disappointed the two youngsters were. The girl with brown curly hair, clutching her money-box, looked close to tears. Who would have thought that old football would have fetched anything?

'Look, there he goes,' said Amy bitterly. 'I hate him.'

'He must have got out pretty quickly,' exclaimed Mini in surprise.

They'd just collected their cycles. Riding ahead of them, through the abbey close, was old Flat-cap. He was rather funny-looking, his huge raincoat, looking as though it had come from a jumble sale, flapping around his bicycle wheels. There was a knapsack on his back which no doubt contained his precious football.

'Let's follow him!' said Mini. 'And see where he lives!'

'What good would that do?' asked Amy, in despair. She was still trembling a bit and in a state of shock. Nearly to have spent all that money, nearly to have recovered the football. Now finding no money spent, no football recovered. What alarming things auctions were!

'Well, you never know. Perhaps if we told him the whole story . . .?' suggested Mini. She was tenacious by nature. She never gave up. 'Perhaps if we begged him? Oh, I dunno. Come on. At least we can find out where the ball ends up.'

Flat-cap seemed in a terrible rush. He was positively fleeing. The girls had to pedal flat out, not to lose sight of him. Over Abbey Bridge he went, then by the cycle-track along The Waterfront, raincoat flapping. When he reached Packers Bridge, he turned right down Bridge Street.

'He lives on our side of town, then,' panted Amy.

'Look!' hissed Mini, when they were well down Bridge Street and JVJ came in sight. 'He's turning down Back Lane!'

Their road!

'How funny,' said Amy. 'Who is he?'

'Never seen him before,' puffed Mini.

They turned right at the school and free-wheeled along Back Lane, cautiously. The figure ahead of them was slowing down, looking at the houses. Then, finally, he braked.

'*Look!*' gasped Amy, in amazement. 'He's stopped.'

Right outside the Knoll House.

He dropped his bike, took off his knapsack and pulled out the football. Then he crept furtively through the front gate and bent down behind the hedge.

'*He seems to be putting the football under our hedge!*' whispered Amy in total bewilderment.

The girls cruised up to the front gate, braked and dismounted. Wide-eyed, they wheeled their bikes through the gate. The stooping figure behind the hedge straightened up. The football was no longer in his hands but tucked under the bottom of the hedge.

They stared at him and he stared back. It wasn't a man at all, just a boy. He hadn't wanted anyone to recognize him at the auction. But the girls recognized him now.

Amy thought how silly he looked, in his

oversized coat, wearing that stupid cap.
He looked pale and frightened, she
thought, with rivulets of sweat running
down his face.

But Mini gazed at him in awe. Sheer,
uncomprehending awe. Fancy him doing
this for them! He'd found out about the
auction, then? Gone along incognito – a
knight in shining armour. He'd decided to
perform a good deed. A beautiful, golden
deed!

'Howard,' breathed Mini. 'You've
brought us our ball back?'

His face contorted with fury.

'Your friends said there'd be nobody here! They said I could just leave it!'

As the girls backed away in astonishment, he took a flying kick at the ball. A really hard kick. Straight at Mini's bike. The bike crashed over, knocked clean from her hands.

'Here! *Have* your ball back! I hope you're satisfied!'

'My bike!' yelled Mini furiously.

Howard Kipps rushed out of the gate then, bending to pick his own bike up. The flat cap fell off and revealed the golden hair. He picked the cap up, rolled it up and shook it at them.

'I've kept my part of the bargain, make sure your friends keep theirs!' he hissed. 'Tell them it's taken my whole month's allowance to get that disgusting old ball back. *A whole month's!*'

He got on his bike and rode off home. 'How was I supposed to know it was somebody's family heirloom?' he screamed over his shoulder.

chapter 11

Hands Up!

'**I**t's not here, Lu!' exclaimed Ben agitatedly. 'It's definitely not here. Is it, Tim?'

Night had fallen but there was a good moon shining on the front garden of the Knoll House. Ben, Tim and Ludo had come crashing up through the back way, straight from David Marshall's party. They'd run to the front and then straight over to the yew hedge. They were totally confident they'd find the football waiting there.

Mini and Amy had been listening out for them and when they heard them go by, they slipped out of the kitchen door and followed. The girls were now hiding behind the bay tree at the corner of the house, watching and listening.

Handles had scurried along the hedge several times, back and forth, bent double,

hunting for the ball. Now they stood in a group, looking very dejected.

'The plan didn't work after all, Lu,' Ben said in despair.

'But it *must* have done,' frowned Ludo. 'Howard Kipps was scared stiff. He definitely swallowed our story didn't he? About how we'd met two of our friends who'd actually seen him do it! Who'd been practising gym against the wall and looked over and *seen* him put it in one of the bags of garden rubbish.' Ludo was rather proud of the ingenious story they'd made up. 'He was scared silly, you could tell!'

'Well, seeing the ball isn't here, we'll have to do what we promised!' said Tim furiously. 'Tell on him to the rector and how precious the ball is with that old footballer's signature on.'

'But the plan *must* have worked,' Ludo repeated.

Ludo was deeply puzzled. It was his plan, after all. From the moment he realized that someone was going to have to bid for the ball at an auction, he'd decided it ought to be Howard Kipps and no one else! He'd told Tim at the fish and chip shop and Ben a little bit later. They'd agreed his idea was brilliant. Ringing up Minster Juniors and discovering that the old ball was signed had given them useful extra ammunition too. It had been extremely satisfying to go and confront the rector's son with his crime. Of course, Howard hadn't admitted his guilt – not for one moment. But it was obvious he was very scared and would be going to that auction, all right. So what had gone wrong?

'Maybe we shouldn't have risked it,' said Ben. 'Maybe we should have let the girls go, after all.'

'Maybe,' muttered Tim uneasily.

'Yes, maybe we should have done,' said Ludo, pale now and feeling responsible.

Amy and Mini looked at those crestfallen faces and could bear it no longer. The boys, they decided, had suffered enough!

They came running out into the moonlit garden.

'What makes you think you could stop us going?' demanded Amy. She threw something up into the air. 'Here, Ben – catch!'

Ben caught Charlie's football and gazed at it in wonder.

'Amy! Mini! Brilliant!' he gasped.

It was rather kind of the boys. They'd brought some lovely food back from the party, for the girls. They were planning to lay on a little feast for them at HQ. They hoped the iced sponge-cakes and delicious little sausage rolls would not only help celebrate the return of the football, but soften the blow when they confessed to the girls what they'd done.

After all, it was bound to be a terrible blow, the truth about Howard. Especially to Mini.

Of course, the feast in the caravan took place anyway.

'If only you'd told us!' said Amy, as she savoured the pink icing on one of the little cakes. 'It would have spared us so much agony.' She shuddered. 'It was terrifying. I never want to go to an auction again. We just thought maybe you meant it, about your principles.'

'Well, we did,' protested Tim. 'Those as well. I mean, give money to *Minster Juniors*?'

'But you should have *told* us,' repeated Mini.

'We just knew you wouldn't believe us,' said Tim. 'About Howard Kipps.'

'We thought . . .' Ludo looked at Mini in embarrassment. 'Well, we thought you really liked him.'

'Who, me?' said Mini indignantly. 'Like *him*?'

'Did you really bid *fourteen pounds*, Amy?' asked Ben disapprovingly.

'Yes! We got really carried away!' nodded Amy. She still trembled slightly when she thought about it. 'I just kept putting my hand up. I had no idea who we were bidding against.'

'And he'll never know it was us, will he?' said Mini. Then, suddenly, she put her sausage roll down. 'I've just realized!

What a difference it made. I mean, that fat lady dropped out of the bidding at one pound fifty. So if we hadn't gone along, Howard could have got the football back for *two pounds* instead of fourteen pounds fifty!'

'Serves him right!' said Tim scornfully. 'Good job you went!'

'And kept putting your hands up!' grinned Ben.

Handles had been right all along, and they really *did* have everything under control, for once. But at two pounds, Howard Kipps would have got off lightly. It was only thanks to Spouts that he'd been taught the lesson of a lifetime! Between them, they'd done rather well.

'Hands up! That's what I say,' joked Ludo. 'Hands up for ever!'

And they all laughed then, even Mini. She thought how nice the boys looked in their best shirts, with their hair brushed and combed for once.

Tim let Harry hold the football on Sunday morning and told him again that he was a clever boy. He might be a brilliant detective one day. He might be allowed to join Handles & Spouts.

'Bootfall in tree!' Harry stated.

Mini's mother decided to take Amy and Mini to church. Reverend Kipps gave a kindly and wise sermon about the importance of looking below the surface of things and not being taken in by appearances.

Mini stared at the golden-haired boy in the choir stalls and whispered to Amy that she agreed with the rector.

It really was a family heirloom.

On Monday, Handles & Spouts got to JVJ early in order to meet Charlie Smith straight off the bus. His face had been pressed to the window, pale and scared-looking. As Ben held up the ball to show him, the boy's eyes nearly popped out with relief.

Now at last, the agony over, he agreed to explain things. He was very shamefaced about it.

The football belonged to his grandmother. She lived in the same village as Charlie and Joe Jackson had been her brother. He'd left her the ball in his will. It was the one used in a famous England victory long ago, when Joe had scored the winning goal.

Charlie's gran treasured the ball. She kept it in a bag in the kitchen cupboard. She'd always forbidden Charlie to play with it, or even touch it, although one day it would be his. 'After I'm gone, Charlie,' she said. 'You'll be old enough to look after it properly then, won't you?'

But Charlie was fed up with waiting – and never having a football to take to school. Last week, while visiting his gran, he'd secretly nicked it. It was only going to be for the day, he explained. Just to have it to bring to JVJ for one day.

But it had all turned out horribly. He'd realized he couldn't tell anyone how special the ball was and how his great-uncle Joe had played for England. Word might have got back to his gran! So the boys in his class had just laughed at it, and they were right. It didn't even kick properly.

Then, horror of horrors, it had stoved in . . . and gone over the wall . . . and got lost.

'But now you've found it and it's cleaned up and all right again!' he said happily. 'Now I can put it back in Gran's cupboard. I know she hasn't found out yet! But I like the new one you got me much

better,' he confided. 'I'll be able to get it out of the bag tonight and then I can bring it to school every day!'

'You'll be really proud of the old one, one day, Charlie,' smiled Ben.

'You won't ever tell no one what I did?' he pleaded. 'You *can* keep a secret? All of you?'

Handles & Spouts nodded. Of course they could keep a secret. They had one of their own.

Mini thought about Howard Kipps during assembly and decided she'd gone right off the idea of joining the church choir.

As for the town's Junior Orchestra, it was a great relief when she heard the news on Wednesday. Howard had got into the Senior one and wouldn't be coming to theirs any more.